MORAG HOOD

WHEN GRANDAD
WAS A PENGUIN

TW🦉 HOOTS

Last time I went to stay
with Grandad, he seemed
a little different.

He talked a lot about fishing.

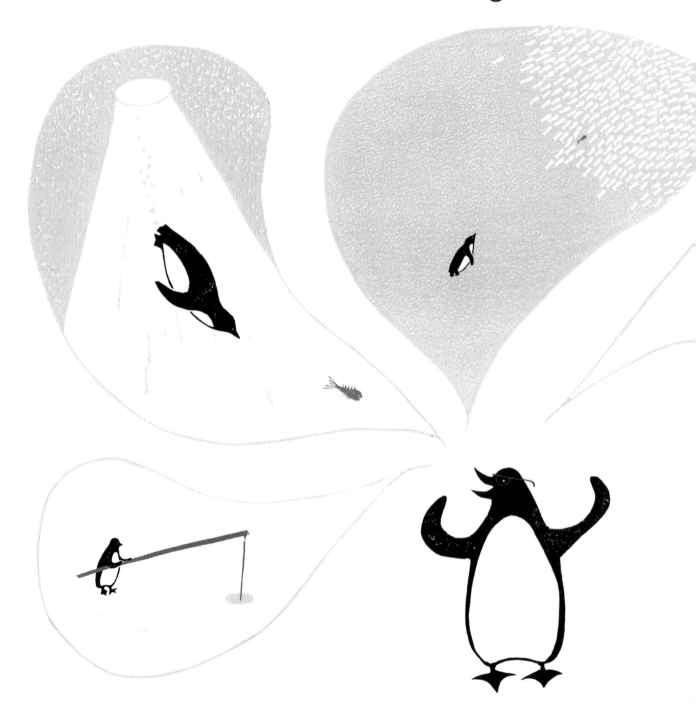

His clothes didn't fit so well,

and he spent a lot of
time in the bathroom.

Perhaps he was just
getting older,

but I kept finding him in
the strangest places.

It was all a
bit fishy.

Then one day
the zoo called.

"I think there may have been a bit of a mix-up."

So we went to the zoo to sort it out.

The penguin went back to
the penguin enclosure . . .

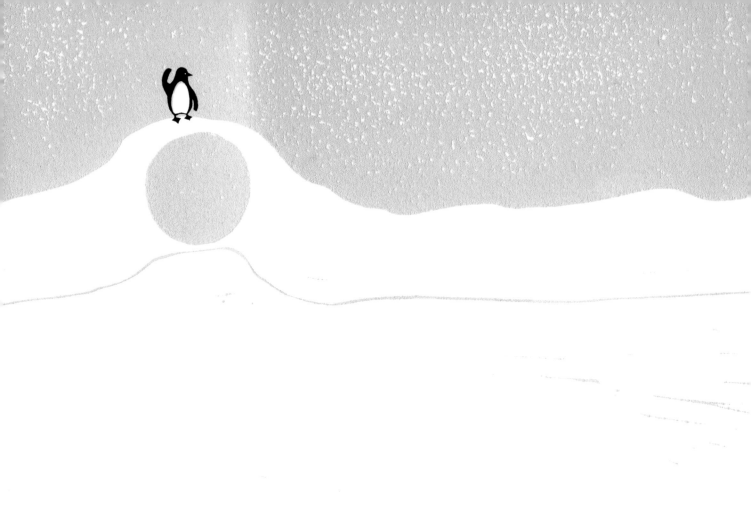

. . . and Grandad came home with me.